# My New Shoes

Lisa Bruce & Susie Jenkin-Pearce

## W
## FRANKLIN WATTS
LONDON•SYDNEY

"Keep still, Bobby. I can't get your shoes on."

297073.

This book is to be returned on or before the last date stamped below.

P1-3.

"Ow, Mummy, I think my shoes have shrunk!"

"You mean your feet have grown too big."

"Come on, Bobby," said Mum.
"It's time for new shoes."

Bobby liked the shoe shop. All the shoes were shiny and new.

"What's the man doing?"
Bobby asked.

"He is measuring your feet," Mum explained, "to find out what size you are."

"Ah ha!" smiled the shop assistant. "You are a size seven."

The man pointed to the racks.
"Which shoes would you like
Bobby?"

Bobby tried on red shoes, blue shoes, shoes with laces and shoes with buckles.

But his favourite were the green shoes. "I like these best."

The shop assistant pressed down on the toe to make sure that the shoes fitted properly.

"They're fine. Now can you walk over to the mirror, please?"

The new shoes were perfect.
"Can I wear them now?"
asked Bobby.

"I'll put your old shoes in a box for you," smiled the shop assistant.

Bobby waved goodbye.
He felt proud of his new shoes.
"Bye," said the man, "see you again."

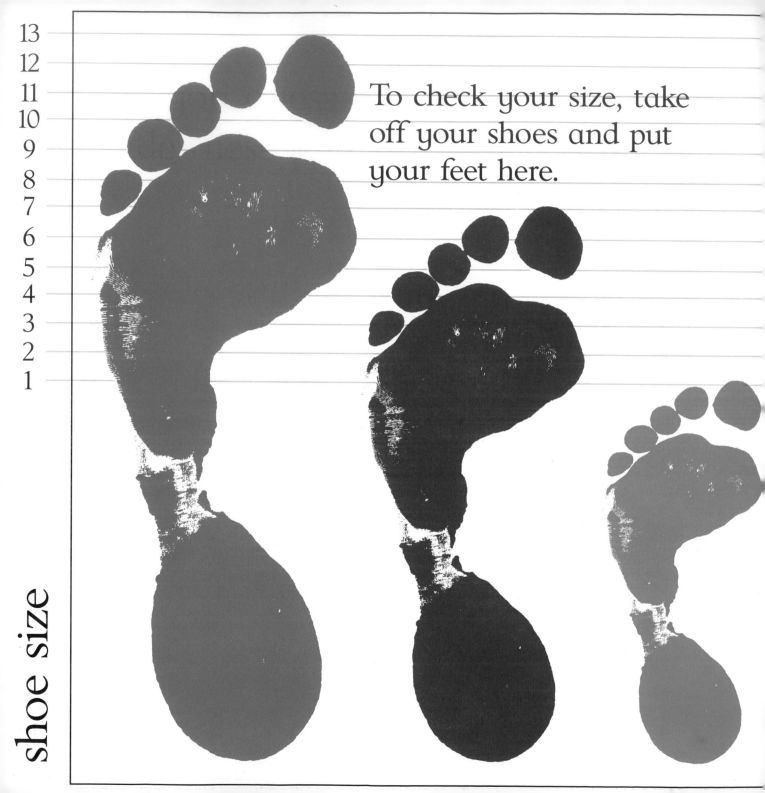

shoe size

13
12
11
10
9
8
7
6
5
4
3
2
1

To check your size, take off your shoes and put your feet here.

Remember you still have to get your feet measured properly in the shoe shop.

13
12
11
10
9
8
7
6
5
4
3
2
1

shoe size

# Sharing books with your child

**Me and My World** are a range of books for you to share with your child. Together you can look at the pictures and talk about the subject or story. Listening, looking and talking are the first vital stages in children's reading development, and lay the early foundation for good reading habits.

Talking about the pictures is the first step in involving children in the pages of a book, especially if the subject or story can be related to their own familiar world. When children can relate the matter in the book to their own experience, this can be used as a starting point for introducing new knowledge, whether it is counting, getting to know colours or finding out how other people live.

Gradually children will develop their listening and concentration skills as well as a sense of what a book is. Soon they will learn how a book works: that you turn the pages from right to left, and read the story from left to right on a double page. They start to realize that the black marks on the page have a meaning and that they relate to the pictures. Once children have grasped these basic essentials they will develop strategies for "decoding" the text such as matching words and pictures, and recognising the rhythm of the language in order to predict what comes next. Soon they will start to take on the role of an independent reader, handling and looking at books even if they can't yet read the words.

Most important of all, children should realize that books are a source of pleasure. This stems from your reading sessions which are times of mutual enjoyment and shared experience. It is then that children find the key to becoming real readers.

This edition 2003

Franklin Watts
96 Leonard Street,
London EC2A 4XD

Franklin Watts Australia
45-51 Huntley Street
Alexandria NSW 2015

ISBN 0 7496 4918 6

A CIP catalogue record for this book is available from the British Library
Dewey Classification 649

First published as *New Shoes* in the Early Worms series

Printed in Belgium

Consultant advice: Sue Robson and Alison Kelly,
Senior Lecturers in Education,
Faculty of Education, Early Childhood Centre,
Roehampton Institute, London.